Picking

The Bones

A Collection of
Tales in the Folk Tradition

Margaret Holbrook

i

This book is dedicated to Grandma Clutterbuck
whose gift for telling tales made an impression on all her
grandchildren, and without whom my delight in the
spoken word of folk tales and legend may not have been
ignited. Thank you.

ABOUT THIS BOOK.

Folk tales are probably the oldest form of storytelling.
These nine stories are written in that tradition.
They are by turn amusing, fantastic and magical.
Animals and plants talk, magic abounds and you have to
believe it; it's there in black and white. It doesn't seem
to matter whether the tales are light and sprinkled with
humour or are written with a darker side, they are certain
to entertain.

Also by Margaret Holbrook

Watching and other Stories
Cul De Sac Tales
Hobby Horses Will Dance

CONTENTS

CROW SONG   1

BLACKER THAN THE NIGHT   7

THE OAK TREE   13

BY THE BRIGHT-POOL WATER   23

THE BOY, THE FARMER
AND THE CAT   35

THE SHEPHERD GIRL   43

THE ORPHAN CHILD   57

THE SEVEN STONES   67

MIRROR, MIRROR   79

CROW SONG

CROW SONG

For seven years she'd watched them. Watched as they raised their young. Watched the chicks grow from awkward, gawky balls of blackness. Watched them as they left the nest and fledged.

For seven years she'd watched all this, watched as the adult pair flew together for the rest of the year. Partners. For seven years she watched all this and thought how lovingly he groomed his mate. Groomed his mate until her feathers shone in the sunlight.

She knew the call that was his above all the birds. She knew his walk and his white-marked tail feather and she wondered whether it was age, this greyness.

For seven years she waved her husband off to work. Watched him drive to the end of the road.

Watched him turn the corner and vanish out of sight as she stood and waved. For seven years she did this. She was sure and never missed a day.

In the autumn of the seventh year she waved to her husband. She watched and waved until he disappeared from sight. Then she looked upward and saw the crow on the roof. He was cawing and bowing as if to her and he was alone. And she watched him, heard his call and saw that he was picking moss from between the roof slates. And all the time she watched. And all the time he was alone.

The sky was dark but split with light, as some autumn mornings are. He was lit in the brightness of the shards and he watched her. He watched her as she closed the door and went into her house. He was alone and she was alone. He knew all this because for seven years he'd watched her. He knew her wave, he knew the soft sound of her voice; knew that she loved autumn best of all the seasons.

For seven years he had watched her.

Later, and when evening began to fall she heard his call as he flew across the sky to his roost. Other birds called but it was his call that she knew and she listened. And then she watched until he disappeared from view. Watched as he hid himself amongst the tall trees whose branches offered little shelter. The tall trees whose winter coat was almost cast and who gave little shelter to him. Up in the tall trees he cawed. He cawed and he watched her.

4

For seven nights he watched her. And she saw him fly to roost. For seven nights after seven years he watched her. And she was alone and he was alone.

And in the morning and for seven more mornings he watched her. Watched her as she stood by the door and waved to her husband. And as he watched her he cawed and she saw him and smiled. And he picked moss from the slates on the roofs and he took the moss he had gathered to the tall trees and there he lined a nest with the soft, green moss. And he was alone.

And after seven mornings it was done. And he watched as she waved, but this morning she didn't go inside. Not today, not on this day. On this day she watched and she waited and she heard him call. So she stood and waited and he came down the path and his feathers were purple black in the morning sun and he called to her as he stood on the path. And she watched him. And she saw that he was as a man. And she stepped down the path and she went to him and he said her name and she knew it, even though it was just his call. The call he had used for seven years and seven nights and seven days. And he was as tall as a man and he took her in his wings. The black purple wings that shone in the sunlight. And she went with him. And her husband lost her. But she watched her husband, still. And she called to him, but he never knew her call or that it was her. He never knew that it was she watching him, and flying past overhead as he turned the corner and disappeared from sight.

BLACKER THAN THE NIGHT

BLACKER THAN THE NIGHT

It is at that point between daylight and the first nudging of night they appear. They dot the sky. Their form like black ink spots on the purple haze.

Some say they will get fast in your hair if they fly too close. Others say *'No. They would never do that. For they have magic in their wings.'*

Older folk who've seen much of these leather winged creatures say they are evil. Say that beasts of the night are not to be trusted. Say that they are creatures of the devil. And then there are those who believe as they are told, and then those who care not a fig for the words they listen to.

Some say that if they catch a girl alone in the dusk-light, corner her away from any other of the human race, then she is lost, forever. She wouldn't stand a chance, and she would belong to them. Belong with their family forever. She'd never know her own family again, nor they her. She would be lost.

And all this could happen within the blink of an eye. It could happen so fast as that, you wouldn't see it. Your girl-child would be gone, disappeared and nothing could save her. Nothing. Even the knowledge of the wise woman, that would be no good. It would be useless against them. Hadn't the wise woman lost her own daughter that very way? And there was nothing that she could know or learn that was enough to bring her back. Nothing. So she lost her.

It was just as her daughter would turn sixteen that she was taken. A girl of such beauty and innocence; and one that would have made any man a fine wife. And she was pleasant of manner too, and tidy and neat about her person. And she kept the house well for her parents, and she could cook and sew, and there was not a person round about that would say anything bad about her. Everyone liked her. And her name was Ruby. And her father had chosen that name for her, and she was as bright as a jewel and they loved her; her mother and father. But even so, the wise woman and her husband lost her.

Ruby's father searched for her. But no one had seen her in the village or in the town. She had vanished. She was gone; lost.

There's some say as it broke her father's heart. And to be sure it did, for he died by his own hand not three months after. And the only one who saw him was the moon. The only one who knew anything was the moon. And the moon was silent.

And Ruby's mother, the wise woman, her heart was broken too. And sixteen years on she is still full with the grief of her troubles. Sixteen years on and she isn't healed. Her heart will not mend. And the sixteen years have taken her to an old woman. An old woman whose hope is gone and all used up; the wise woman who couldn't save her own daughter.

She has nothing now except her house and her dog. And the dog is her family. And she is his. And the dog will not leave. Not to be taken like her daughter and her husband. And the wise woman knows this. The wise woman knows she will not be alone, that the dog will not leave her. And the dog is pleased because she is his family and feeds him well and cares for him. And bats do not take dogs. They fly away from dogs and that is the way it is and that is the way it will always be. Because that is how it was meant, and the wise woman knows this. So, even though her grief is no less and her heart is not happy, even so, she is content.

THE OAK TREE

THE OAK TREE

By the house in the wood where Geraldine had lived for more than twenty years there was an oak tree. The tree had grown with her, babe to child, child to girl, girl to woman. It was a special tree, her father had said. It was a tree with powers, and her father had looked after it well.

It was a Sessile oak, he told her. And she remembered this. And Geraldine knew the oak, talked to it as her father had done. To make it grow, to nurture it.

Geraldine remembered all the things her father had taught her, everything. And now she was alone, (her parents dead these last six years) she carried on in the ways of her parents and talking to the tree as her father had done, and nurturing it. The tree, you see, was her only companion.

No one else lived within a half days journey of the cottage, there was no company. The tree was her company and her friend. Her only friend.

When it was market day in the nearby town, Geraldine would set off before dawn to take her goods and trade them. She made buttons for the fancy frocks of the townsfolk. She made buttons from bone and silk and wood, and the people in the town would wait for Geraldine to come each market day with her buttons; for they knew her work, and they knew they were the best. Geraldine traded her buttons for food and other goods she might need for the coming week. Geraldine didn't keep livestock, buttons were her only trade. And she had no pack animals. There was no mule to carry stock and goods for her. Everything she took to town and everything she brought back must be carried by her, and she did it, this carrying, as she had done when she was a girl and had made the journey with her father. She did it, but still found the task hard, the journey long. And in the winter when the days were short and the nights would come too soon, then it almost broke her. Then, it was almost too much.

The only constant companion in this life of toil was the oak tree. And though she talked to him and nurtured him, he was indifferent.

Geraldine tried to fathom the tree, but though they had grown together, from child to woman, from acorn to oak, they were of different worlds.

One morning in the spring of the year as Geraldine was setting off for market, she said goodbye to the tree, as she always did. This day though, she thought she heard a sound. She thought that she heard the tree speak. For a moment she studied the tree, regarded it in a way she had never done before, and then she noticed something. She noticed that one of the branches on the oak tree was dying. It was spring. This was the time when the tree should be coming into new life but instead it was dying.

She decided then and there that when she was in town she would see what she could do. She would see if anyone knew how to save the oak tree, her one and constant companion.

Geraldine asked everyone she knew at the market if they could help her save the tree, if they knew a cure that would stop it from dying. Each one she asked gave the same answer. There was no-one who could help her.

Time had gone on. It was getting late. She quickly bought the goods she needed and set off for home.

When she arrived at the cottage she straightaway took her goods inside and then she came back out to look at the tree. It was no better.

'What am I to do?' she said. 'Not one person at the market could help. The people there knew nothing of trees.'

It was quiet in the wood, but Geraldine was certain that she heard a noise, a voice. She looked at the tree.

'Are you trying to talk to me?' she asked, but she heard nothing more. With a backward glance she went into the house to make herself some supper.

The next morning she was up early. She went outside to look at the tree. It was getting worse. A branch at the side of the tree had started to die.

Geraldine stood where she was and began to cry. The tears fell deep and fast and one tear touched the tree.

'Don't die on me. You can't leave me. I can't lose you. You're all I have,' Geraldine said, and she bowed her head and closed her eyes.

After a few moments she thought that she heard the tree make a noise. She looked up.

'Are you speaking?' she asked. But she heard nothing more. All around her was silence. Not even the singing of a bird did she hear. Geraldine realised how alone she was, and the greatness of her loneliness made her sad.

Geraldine returned to the house and her button-making. She had orders for fine silk buttons from one of the tailors in town. It was a full three days work .She would have to work long hours to get them finished and ready for market day.

When she next set off for market she was very tired. She hadn't slept much at all during the last few days and she was exhausted. Such was her tiredness she could hardly put one foot in front of the other. She looked at the oak tree. 'Old Sessile' she said, 'please don't die on me. I have to go to market but I'll have time for you when I get back. I promise.'

'No,' she heard as she turned to leave. Geraldine turned and looked round, startled. There was no one there, only the tree. She studied the tree for a while. The oak looked no different to her. It was still dying. She looked down to the ground, to where she had stood last night and to where her tears had fallen. *Was that a new piece of growth on the tree?* She looked closely and saw a pink, fresh, shoot, low down below one of the dying branches that had now fallen away.

She looked up again and smiled. 'You're going to survive, aren't you? I know it.'

And then Geraldine turned and left for market. Now there was a spring in her step. The day would be brighter after all, she thought.

'These buttons are not of the usual quality. I can only give you half the agreed price. The work is so very poor,' the tailor said.

'It is my usual work and these buttons were especially made for you. I cannot accept half payment. I have to live...and I have to buy more silk.'

'Then you should ensure your work is of the highest quality if you want me to buy it.'

'You're cheating me,' Geraldine replied. 'There is nothing the matter with my work.'

'I think you'd better apologise for what you've just said, or leave.' The tailor said.

Geraldine said not one more word and she turned and left the tailor's shop. She was devastated, but she also knew that she was right. The tailor was trying to trick her.

When she arrived home she had sold only a few buttons, barely enough to buy her food for the week. It seemed the tailor had many friends and that Geraldine had no one.

Before she went inside her home, she stopped and looked at the tree. More leaves were falling from the base. Only this morning she had thought that the tree was recovering, now she wasn't so sure.

Geraldine turned her key in the lock and pushed open the door.

'Ger-al-dine.'

Geraldine turned. She wasn't imagining anything. The tree had just spoken her name.

'Sessile oak. You can speak, but what does all this mean? What is happening?'

She stood for a while and observed the tree. Nothing more was said or heard and Geraldine went inside.

The next week when she prepared to set off for market she was worried. More of the tree was dying and the new shoots were coming to nothing. She was also bothered about the tailor. Would he have passed on more rumour about her and her work? Would she sell enough buttons to be able to buy her food for the week and more silk?

Geraldine's fears were not unfounded. She sold nothing all day. She hadn't a penny piece to carry home. Her life was not worth living.

When she arrived home that evening she went straight inside the house. She never even paused to speak to the oak tree. She looked around her. She'd nothing, nothing at all. Everything in the house belonged to her parents. The house had been theirs. The reason she was living where she was, was because of her parents. The reason her life was so hard was because of her parents. She cried and cried until there were no tears left. And then quietly and methodically she took a case from a cupboard and packed it with the few possessions that she owned. The few things that belonged to her alone, and when she was done and she was ready to leave the home she had known babe to child, child to girl, girl to woman, she went to talk to the oak tree. The tree that had lived by the cottage as long as she had. The tree that was dying.

'Sessile oak, I'm leaving. I'm leaving now, right away before I change my mind. I cannot stay in this place a moment longer. I'm loathe to leave you. You have been my only friend and I'm saddened to say goodbye; but you're dying. I cannot help you. I've tried and I've failed. I won't leave you to die alone. I can't do that. I'm going to chop you down now. I'm going to save you any more pain.'

Geraldine went to the wood-shed at the back of the house and took her father's axe. She came back and started to hack at the base of the tree. Each time she chopped at the base of the tree, the tree cried out, 'Save me.'

'I'm not listening to you. You made me believe I could hear you speak. Well I know there's no one there. It's nothing. A tree can't speak.'

'But I can Geraldine. I can.'

Geraldine looked up from what she was doing and saw a man standing there. A man tall and strong and dressed all in green.

'Who are you?'

'I'm the spirit of the wood, come to life.'

'What does that mean?' she asked.

'You've freed me, Geraldine. Your actions have freed me to be a man again, and for that I thank you.'

'A man again. I don't understand?'

'I was trapped in the oak by a sprite. You have set me free. That's all you need to know.'

21

'I'm pleased that you're happy,' she replied, and then, 'and if you're a man, you will know that I'm leaving. You will know what I've said.'

'I heard you Geraldine, and the choice you have made is a good one. No one should live alone without friend or company.'

'I'm pleased that you agree, though I don't know why.'

'You won't understand yet, but in time you may.'

'That sounds rather like a riddle to me.'

'I'll explain as we walk on. As we walk along together. No one should ever be alone.'

BY THE BRIGHT POOL WATER

BY THE BRIGHT POOL WATER

In this place, by the river, is where she always sat when she'd time to take a break from being a serving-girl. But Mabs wasn't any ordinary serving-girl, Mabs had powers, magic powers and the powers came from the bright-pool water.

No one at *The Harp and Goat's Horn*, knew this; although they often wondered how she finished the jobs she'd been tasked to do, so quickly, and she was quick. No more than the blink of an eye and the lodging rooms were cleared, ready for the next travellers, no more than a gentle wink and the boards and flagons were cleaned and ready for the next customers.

'What are you doing, Mabs?' She turned to see Cedric, the inn-keeper's son watching her.

'Nothing, just thinking.'

'Why is your hand in the water, and why is there a strange light glowing all around?'

'It's a hot afternoon. I just wanted to feel the coolness on my skin. And the glow? I don't know what you're talking about. There is no glow. It must be the light playing tricks on you. Come on, sit down next to me. You can feel the water, put your hand in the pool, don't be afraid, there's nothing to bite you!'

'I'll sit for a while, but I'm not getting wet. I don't like it. I don't care for water, not at all.'

'What a thing to say! You drink and wash don't you? And for that you must use water.'

Cedric laughed. 'Don't mock me Mabs, of course I wash and drink, but, promise not to tell of my fear of water.'

'I promise, cross my heart and hope to die, and anyway it's only your hand you're going to put into the water, not your whole body.'

'I know, but it's the not knowing what lies beneath, that's my fear.'

Cedric sat down next to Mabs and rolled up his sleeve, and then, very gingerly, he put his hand into the bright-pool water.

'It's not as bad as you thought, eh?' Mabs said. Cedric smiled and then they began to talk of life and work and what they wanted to do with the rest of their lives. They chatted pleasantly for some time and then Cedric said, 'Where are your parents, Mabs?'

'They took to travelling when I was young. When they could no longer provide for me they left me at *The Harp and Goat's Horn*, left me on the doorstep.

Thankfully for me your mother took pity on me and cared for me until I was old enough to work.'

'She doesn't work you too hard, my mother?'

'I work no more and no less than the other girls. Your mother treats us all fairly.'

'Good, that's good to know.' Cedric got up.

'Are you going all ready?' Mabs asked.

'I must. There'll be casks to get down into the cellar and the yard will need sweeping.'

'I'm staying here a little while longer. It's so peaceful.'

Cedric left and Mabs stayed where she was until she saw that Cedric had disappeared from view. When she was sure that he was no longer in sight she took her hand from the water and dried it on her dress. She pointed upward with her index finger and a bolt of lightning shot from her finger-tip.

That's good, my energy's restored, she thought. And she got up and began walking slowly back to the tavern. She hadn't been walking for very long when Cedric jumped out from the trees and stood on the path in front of her, blocking her way.

'Cedric!' she said, 'you startled me. I thought you'd be back at the tavern by now.'

'I was watching you,' Cedric said, 'and I saw what you did with your hand. You caused a bolt of lightning to flash through the sky.'

'You must be dreaming, Cedric. I did no such thing. Now come on, let's get back to the tavern. I have work to do and your father will be wondering where we are.'

'That would be good for you, wouldn't it, if we could just forget it. But no, I'm afraid I can't do that. You're not getting away with it that easily, Mabs. I know what I saw. Now, we're not going anywhere until you tell me how you did it. You tell me how you made the lightning strike and then I'll move out of your path and let you go home.'

'You're being silly Cedric. There's nothing to tell,'

'You have magic powers. I saw it just now. I saw what you did. We've thought for a long time that you were different. How else do you get your work at the tavern finished so quickly, tell me that?'

'I have no magic powers. You're making things up, now let me pass.'

'I've told you Mabs, I'll let you pass when you tell me where you get your powers from. I've seen them; I know what you can do.'

'All right, Cedric, but you must promise not to tell anyone. It must be our secret.'

'Promise.'

'Right, come back with me to the bright-pool water.'

'I've told you, I don't like water.'

'And I'm telling you that's where I get my powers from. You want the powers, don't you?' Mabs said this knowing that the water would have no effect at all on Cedric. For one thing, you had to be born to the magic to own the powers. I t had to be there in your past, and whichever way you looked at it, Cedric was definitely not born to it. And the second thing, you had to be the seventh daughter of a seventh daughter, which

Mabs was; or the seventh son of a seventh son, and
Cedric again, most definitely was not.

Cedric stood looking at Mabs.

'You are coming with me?' Mabs asked.

'Yes.'

'Well, come on then.'

They walked for a few minutes until they were
back at the bright-pool water.

'Sit down next to me,' Mabs said, 'and do as you
did before. It didn't harm you then and it won't harm
you now.'

Cedric did as he was told.

'Now,' Mabs said, 'move your hand slowly back
and forth, you will feel a warmth as the water runs over
your hand, keep doing it until you feel the warmth.
When your hand feels warm, then you know that the
powers are working. Keep on doing it until you can feel
the heat come from your hand and up into your arm.
When the warmth has reached the top of your arm it is
time to bring your hand out of the water.'

'Is that why you come to the pool so often?'
Cedric asked.

'How do you know how often I come to the
water, have you been watching me?'

'Of course. You do not think it was by chance
that I turned up today, do you? I watch everything you
do. I have seen you blink your eyes to tidy the
bedchambers, and blink to clean the boards and flagons.'

'That is something no one should ever do, watch
a person so intently. It is wrong Cedric, very wrong.'

'I only did it because I wanted to know all about you. I am twenty-one now, and a man. I have to be thinking about taking a wife. I would like you to be my wife, Mabs.'

'I cannot be your wife. I am so much older than you, so much older than you will ever know.'

'You are lying to me. We played together as children. I know you are only a few years older than I am.'

'I do not lie to you Cedric. I am old; older than your mother and your grandmother. It is the pool that keeps me young, and while I come here every day, I stay young.'

'You must be mad! It cannot be! You are lying to me, you must be.'

'I am not lying. If you do not believe me, come back tomorrow and see me for what I really am.'

'What do you mean?'

'If you come back tomorrow I will be here and I will not put my hand into the water. You can stay and watch as I age before your eyes.'

'It cannot be, you are lying.'

'Come back tomorrow and you will see.'

Cedric got up from the pool, dried off his arm and began walking back to the tavern. Mabs stayed where she was. As night began to fall she decided she had been away from the tavern for long enough and began her walk back. It was late when she arrived back at the tavern and so she crept up to her room that was at the top of the building. She lay down on her bed and fell asleep.

In the morning she was up bright and early and had done all her jobs before eleven o'clock. She was just getting ready to go to the pool when Cedric's father called to her. 'We missed you last evening. Matilda and Ann had to do your work. You can stay here today and serve. Let them have some time off.'

'Oh, but I can't. I'm meeting someone.'

'Well they'll just have to wait, won't they?'

'But, if I stay, something might happen to me.'

'You're talking in riddles now girl. Just get to the kitchen and help Hannah with the food, and be ready to serve when the customers start coming in.'

'If I must.'

At half past twelve the tavern was a hive of activity. Mabs did as she was told and served ale and brought out food as it was ordered. At half past one the trade was still brisk. Mabs looked at the tavern-keeper.

'Please, I know it's busy, but may I go out, just for half an hour?'

'No. How can I let you go now? You can see how busy we are. I need you here, and if you want time off, you should be better with your time-keeping. I can't pay you and do the work myself.'

'I don't feel well, I'll have to sit down,' Mabs said.

'No you won't, not while we've got customers coming in who want to be served.'

Mabs went through to the kitchen to help Hannah. After a few minutes work she said, 'Hannah, can you manage if I just go out? I'll only be half an hour?'

'What if the master comes in? What then?'

'Tell him I've gone to the well to bring water. He'll believe you.'

'All right. But please be as quick as you can.'

'I will.'

Mabs set off as quickly as she could to get to the bright-pool water. When she was there, she saw Cedric waiting. She looked at her hands; they were wrinkled and marked with the brown spots of age. She put her hand to her face. Her skin was dry and she could feel the wrinkles that lined her face. She knew that Cedric would never believe that it was she. That he would never believe that she was this old woman.

Mabs began walking towards Cedric. Her voice croaked as she began to speak. 'Cedric, I'm here.'

Cedric turned and saw the old hag in front of him.

'Who are you?' He asked.

'It's me, Mabs. The girl you asked to marry you last evening.'

'Go away, don't be foolish. The Mabs I know is young.'

'The Mabs you know told you she was old, older than your mother and grandmother. How would I know that if it wasn't because I spoke the words with my own lips.'

'But it can't be!'

'But it is. Watch now as I put my hand into the pool.'

Cedric watched, and in a few moments Mabs was standing in front of him, exactly as he remembered.

'This is some sort of trickery. Go away, and leave me alone.'

'I am going Cedric, back to the tavern, back to my work.'

When Mabs arrived back at the tavern, Hannah was waiting for her.

'The master's been looking for you; you'd better get out the front and serve. It's busy out there.'

'Thanks Hannah, but I'm going now, leaving for good. If the master comes, you tell him that. And tell him I shan't be coming back either. And Cedric, tell him that I'll miss him, but that it was best he know the truth.'

'I will, but it makes no sense to me.'

'And nor should it, but in a year or two, you'll make master Cedric a good wife, just remember that.'

And Mabs pointed her hands to the ceiling, and from her index fingers shot a bolt of blue, and she was gone. And to this day no one knows where she went, for no one ever saw her again; but two years later Hannah and Cedric were married, and as they came from the church a bolt of blue shot from the sky, and for a second they both thought that they had seen Mabs, but it was only for a fleeting second, and neither mentioned anything of it to the other.

THE BOY, THE FARMER AND THE CAT

THE BOY, THE FARMER AND THE CAT

George, the farmer's boy always drove the cart to market on Friday. He had done so for the past three years.

He took the grain the farmer grew. It was always seventeen sacks George took to market. The farmer would tell him the price to charge. George would sell the oats and then return home later in the day, all the grain sold, and give the farmer his money.

George could be trusted and that was all the farmer wanted, someone who was trustworthy.

George, for his part, was a simple soul. Working for the farmer was the only work he had. George wished that he could be rich, like the people he heard about in stories, but as much as he wished, his wishes never came true.

One Friday evening, when George had returned from the market and the farmer had paid him, a strange thing occurred. A cat that happened to be walking across the farmyard, stopped, right in front of George.

'So, you want to be rich?' the cat said.

George blinked. He wasn't so simple as to believe in talking cats. He side-stepped, to get around the cat.

'So, you don't want to be rich?' the cat asked.

George turned and looked at the cat.

'Yes, it is me who's speaking to you,' the cat said.

'Cats don't talk,' George answered.

'No, not all cats talk, but I do,' the cat replied.

'I see,' said George.

'But you don't,' said the cat, 'that's why you ignored me.'

'Well, tell me then,' said George, 'how I can become rich.'

'Well, first you have to listen and do exactly as I tell you,' said the cat.

'Tell me then,' George replied.

'Next Friday when you take the grain to market charge two pennies more than the price the farmer tells you. That money will be yours.'

'But that's stealing,' George replied.

'No it isn't,' said the cat, 'The farmer barely pays you for the work you do, and besides, later on you will be able to help him. Just do as I say. You will keep the money and you will buy a ram.'

'A ram?'

'A ram,' replied the cat.

'Why would I buy a ram?' George asked.

'You want to buy a ram to start your flock.'

'I will have to buy some grain for the ram, to feed it, otherwise it will die.'

'No, it won't die, nor will you need to buy grain,' replied the cat, 'it will eat the grass outside your house.'

The next week, George did as he had been told by the cat. He came home that night with a ram. He tethered the ram outside his house, on the grass. It was happy as a king, and started to eat the grass.

The next week as George set off for market with the seventeen sacks of grain, the cat appeared again.

'So, you bought the ram?'

'I did. He's tethered by my house now, and eating the grass.'

'That's good,' said the cat. 'Now today when you take the grain to market, do the same as you did before, but this time, buy a ewe.'

'A ewe?'

'Yes,' replied the cat. 'If you buy a ewe you can put it in with the ram and in late winter, early spring, you will have lambs.'

'I'll only have one or two lambs from one ewe,' George replied.

'Yes, but do the same thing for a few weeks until you have six ewes, and then the lambs you get can be sold at market.'

'But I'm cheating the farmer. It isn't right.'

'It's called investing,' said the cat, 'and soon the money you have will more than pay back the farmer, plus, *you* will have the sheep.'

George felt uneasy about doing this. The farmer was a good man, and George didn't want to lose his job, but that night when George returned home from market he had two ewes. He had done what the cat had said.

For weeks this went on. George soon had so much livestock that he had a small farm of his own. It meant that George had to build pens for the animals, to keep them safe. He was turning into a very busy man.

One day, when George went to deliver the grain to market for the farmer, the farmer said, 'I hear you've sheep now, on your land. Come into some money, have you?'

'In one way,' George replied.

'That's good,' the farmer said. 'I might soon have to be working for you!'

George was surprised, but he just answered, 'You still have grain for me to sell today, don't you?'

'Yes, seventeen sacks as usual.'

George took the grain and set off for market in the cart. Soon the cat jumped up on the cart and turned to face George.

'Your farmer friend's in trouble; and you are doing so well. Charge a third more for the grain and take back four ewes, and the money, and give it all to the farmer.'

'What if he doesn't want sheep?'

'He will,' replied the cat.

That evening when George returned from the market, he gave the farmer the money and the sheep. Just as the cat had said, the farmer was pleased. The farmer built pens for the sheep and said that George must take seventeen more sacks of grain to the market the following day, he must charge the same price and bring back four more ewes.

George did as the farmer asked and he did the same for the following three weeks. Soon the farmer had a small flock of sheep.

A few weeks later, when George turned up to take the farmer's grain to market, the farmer said, 'Sell the grain for four times the price and bring me back eight sheep.'

'I'll try,' George said.

George hadn't gone very far when he was joined by the cat. 'No one will buy the grain. The farmer has become too greedy,' the cat said.

When George reached the market he tried as hard as he could to sell the grain, but no one would buy. The cat was right. The grain price was just too high. George drove home with the seventeen sacks of grain still on the cart. When the farmer saw this he was furious.

'You cannot do a simple task,' he said.

George replied, 'I could have sold the grain, but not for the price you asked. It was too expensive.'

'I'll do the job myself, tomorrow. And you can be gone. I won't have work for you anymore,' the farmer said.

When the farmer took the grain to market he was sure he would be able to sell it, even at a high price, but he was wrong. He returned home with the seventeen sacks. No one was buying. The same thing happened the next day. Soon, the grain wasn't worth anything. It had rotted in the sacks. The farmer had to throw it all away.

A few more weeks went by and the farmer still couldn't sell his grain. No one at all would buy from him now, even when he dropped the price. He went to see George, to offer him his old job back. George said he would work as before, on the one day a week, but he didn't want payment, it would be his gift to the farmer.

Just at that moment, as George and the farmer were talking, the cat came across the farmyard and sat at the feet of the farmer; then he began to speak. The farmer looked bemused and scratched his head.

'Don't think this is a dream,' George said. 'This is really happening and this cat *can* talk. If he tells you to do something, do it.'

The cat was quiet for a while, and then he said,

'Mr Farmer, you know in your heart why things went wrong for you. Your greed took over. If you'd only added a few pence more to the price of your grain, the people would have bought it. But you weren't satisfied. You had to ask four times the usual price, and so you sold nothing. You ended up throwing your grain away and so lost money. Greed was your downfall. Do not let your eagerness to make money cloud your judgement again.

The farmer looked at George and the cat and said, 'That's right. I wanted wealth above all.'

The cat said, 'Wealth is fine, but not at the expense of everything else.' And then the cat stood up, arched his back and walked away. The farmer and George never saw him again.

THE SHEPHERD GIRL

THE SHEPHERD GIRL

On their third meeting, that was when he gave her the
cloak of dawn, and as he draped it around her shoulders
she was transformed. It made her silver-pink, white, gold
and teal-blue. Teal-blue to match her eyes. To him she
became in that moment a princess, and he was pleased.

She did not speak to him. She could not, for her
lips had been mute since birth. She could not tell him
how thankful she was for the beautiful gift, so she kissed
him. Kissed him and then ran away.

He called after her but she ignored him and
carried on running. As she ran faster and faster, ashamed
at what she had just done, she realised she wasn't
wearing the cloak anymore. It had fallen from her
shoulders, and when she looked down she saw that she

was in her shabby every-day clothes. The clothes of a shepherdess; and an impoverished one at that.

Her father looked at her when she returned home, asked her what she was running from, but she could not answer.

'You're damned silly sometimes my girl,' he said, 'you go around with your head in the clouds. Where've you left the sheep? The wolves will catch them and that's all our money gone.'

The girl said nothing, she could not answer, but went back outside and retraced her footsteps back the way she had come; tried to find the cloak, but she could not.

When she was back at her father's field on the hillside, she was pleased to see that all the sheep were safe and well. She counted them and was pleased that they numbered twenty-five. They were all there; she had not lost a one.

She sat down on the cool, soft grass. She had only been there for a few minutes when she saw the young man approaching. She could see that he was carrying the cloak of dawn. Once more he put the cloak around her shoulders. Once more she became transformed into a beautiful princess. A silent princess.

This time she didn't kiss him, she just looked at him, tried to say the words that were in her heart, tried to ask him his name, tried to ask him who he was, but nothing, nothing came from her lips.

'You can't speak, can you?'

The girl shook her head.

'You look after the sheep. Do they belong to your father and mother?'

She nodded and then took a paper and pencil from her pocket and scribbled a few words, *only my father, my mother died.*

The boy took the paper and read it.

'I'm sorry', he said.

The girl looked down and smiled, drew the cloak around her. The sun had begun to go down and the early evening was cool.

'You can keep the cloak,' the boy said, 'I have to go now but I'll come tomorrow, here, and sit with you again.'

The girl smiled, and then waved to the boy as he began his walk into the town. She knew it was time now, for her to settle the sheep for the night, and when that was done, then she could go home. But first the sheep had to be made secure and penned for the night.

'You're late daughter', her father said as she walked in through the door. 'And what's that around you. You've not been thieving have you?'

The girl shook her head, upset that her father could think such a thing.

Her father smiled at her. 'That's all right then. Now you'd better go and make the supper. I'm hungry even if you're not.'

The girl took the cloak off and hung it up on a hook by the door and then went into the kitchen that was at the back of the cottage. She had prepared the vegetables before she had left to go and tend the sheep, and there was some cold meat on a plate from the evening before. Soon the girl and her father were eating.

'A good meal you've made for us tonight,' her father said.

The girl looked at her father and smiled. She could not answer him. If she could she would have told him how much she cared for him and that she wished he could treat her more kindly. They only had each other. He shouldn't be harsh to her.

Then the girl cleared the dishes away. Only when this final task was done could she rest. When the girl had cleared everything away she came out of the kitchen. Her father was sitting in his chair by the hearth, smoking his pipe. She went over to him and kissed him on the forehead. He said, 'Goodnight,' to her. His daughter smiled and went off to bed.

In the morning she was up early and made the breakfast for herself and her father. After she had eaten and cleared everything away, she went and put on her cloak of dawn and then she left to tend the sheep.

It was a beautiful morning and all the way along the path the girl kept thinking about the boy and was hoping that he wouldn't forget his promise to come and sit with her again.

He didn't forget. As the afternoon sun began to set in the sky, he appeared.

'Hello', he said.

The girl just smiled at him.

'I need to know your name,' he said. 'I can't keep calling to visit you and not know your name. You do have a name, don't you?'

The girl nodded and took a paper from her pocket. On it she wrote, 'Meinir,' and gave the note to the boy.

'That's a lovely name. Meinir, thank-you.' He stood for a little while and then he said, 'I have to go now, but I'll visit you again tomorrow. Goodbye Meinir.' And as he said 'goodbye', he took her hand and kissed it, and then he was gone.

When the boy had gone, Meinir realised that she didn't know his name. She would ask him tomorrow.

The next day as evening approached, Meinir sat in her cloak, the cloak that the boy had given her, and waited for him to arrive. Time passed but the boy didn't come.

Meinir drew the cloak of dawn about her to shield herself from the chill, for the evenings were cold. She went about her business, penned up the sheep for the night and set off on her walk home, her lonely walk home. She was sad. She looked at her clothes. She felt like a princess, yet beneath the cloak she was just a poor shepherd-girl. Maybe she wouldn't see the boy again. Maybe he wouldn't visit her. The thought upset her.

When she arrived home she went straight into the kitchen to prepare the meal for her father. The food had been slowly cooking all day and Meinir was glad that there wasn't much to do. Her father never spoke to her as she silently put out the meal.

After they had eaten, he said to her, 'You look tired tonight, daughter. Is something bothering you?'

Meinir shook her head. Her father wouldn't understand, and besides she wanted the boy to be her secret, for now, at least.

Her father never spoke to her again that evening and Meinir quietly, silently, cleared away the things and went to her bed.

In the morning she was up early. She had cleaned the cottage until it shone and she had made the meal ready for the evening. As she was ready to go out to tend the sheep she took her cloak from the hook by the door.

'Daughter, you've given me my breakfast but you've not eaten. Are you taking some food with you? You can't manage all day without food.'

Meinir shook her head, and hurried out of the door. When she arrived at the field, she went to the pen and let the sheep out to graze. The day passed. Soon it was evening. And with the evening Meinir went and penned up the sheep for the night and started her walk home. Again the boy had not visited. Meinir's heart was heavy with sadness.

The next evening as Meinir sat watching the sheep she was so cold that she shivered. She had forgotten the cloak of dawn and her clothes were worn and thin and the cold went through them and her and on into her bones. Every inch of her ached, she was so weary.

After a few more minutes she decided the hour was late enough and she went and collected the sheep and herded them into their pen for the night. Then she turned and began her lonely walk home. Meinir hadn't walked very far when a sudden terror struck her. She felt that she couldn't go on. She couldn't take another step. As weak as she was, she stopped, hoping to regain some strength and finish her journey. She knew that her father would be waiting for her and as harsh as he could sometimes be, she knew that he would be worried about her.

Meinir leant against an oak tree and there she rested for a while, when she felt a little stronger she set off once more, but she only managed a few steps. It was no use, she fell down to the ground in a heap. There seemed to be no life in her. Soon, a warm breeze was blowing through the trees. It became stronger and stronger until it was strong enough to blow the leaves down from the trees. And the leaves covered the girl and kept her warm, and it was like this that she was found.

The boy who had not visited and whose absence had caused her pain was the one who found her. He came by the spot in the woods where she lay. He was on a grand horse and flanked by several other riders and the rider nearest the boy carried a standard.

As soon as the boy saw the girl, he jumped down from his horse, brushed away the leaves that were covering the girl and picked her up and placed her on his horse in front of him. Then they rode together with the other men to the cottage where the girl lived with her father. (The boy had watched the girl as she walked home and knew exactly the path to take through the woods, knew the exact path to the cottage Meinir shared with her father.)

Meinir's father was shocked when he saw how ill his daughter was. He drew a chair to the fireside and brought some blankets and warmed some milk for her to drink. Meinir's father then thanked the boy and his men for bringing his daughter home.

'She cannot tend the sheep tomorrow, she must rest until she is well,' the boy said. 'I will send one of my men and he will tend the sheep for you.'

'How do you know about the sheep?' Meinir's father asked.

'I have watched your daughter many times tending your flock. I am the one who gave her the cloak of dawn.' The boy pointed to where the cloak was hanging.

Meinir's father smiled.

'So you are the one who gave her the cloak,' he said.

'I am. And I would ask something else of you now, sir. I wish to marry your daughter if she will have me.'

Meinir's father laughed in disbelief. 'My daughter is mute, has been since her birth. She's not a girl for making marriage with. She'll stay here and look after me, and then...'

'And then?' The boy asked.

'I don't know what will happen to her when I'm gone.'

'All the better that she marries me then, don't you think?'

'If you say so, I suppose, but as long as you know what you're taking on, that's all.'

'If she agrees, we'll marry,' the boy said.

The boy left and one of his men stayed the night at the cottage. He was to take over Meinir's task of tending the sheep in the morning.

The following day, as the sun was at its height in the sky, and the sky itself without cloud or break, there was a knock at the cottage door. When Meinir's father went to the door and opened it, he saw the boy there.

'How's Meinir?' the boy asked.

'She's resting, but she's still very weak. I must thank you again for allowing one of your men to tend our sheep for us. I could not have managed on my own,' Meinir's father said.

'May I come in?' the boy asked.

Meinir's father stood back and let the boy come into the house. He went straight over to the fireside, to where Meinir was sitting. She smiled when she saw the boy, and she was so pleased that it was he who was their visitor.

'You must put on the cloak I gave you,' the boy said.

'She's warm enough. She doesn't need your cloak, and besides, that cloak is like no fabric I've ever seen. It's so thin that you can almost see through it.'

'That's because it's special,' the boy said.

'Why is it special? It doesn't look special to me,' Meinir's father said.

'It is special. It has magical powers.'

Meinir's father laughed. 'What do you mean? Someone's been filling your head full of nonsense if you believe anything to have magical powers.'

'No one has filled my head with anything. Pass me the cloak, please.'

Meinir's father went and got the cloak. The boy took it and placed it around Meinir's shoulders. At once she became as a princess.

The boy knelt at Meinir's feet.

'Meinir, will you marry me?'

Meinir smiled and nodded.

'No, Meinir, I have to hear it from your lips. You must tell me that you will marry me.'

'I told you last night, the girl can't speak. She's been mute from birth,' her father said.

'Meinir, answer me. Tell me that you will marry me.'

Meinir was silent. Again the boy asked, 'Meinir, tell me that you will marry me.'

Meinir began to cry. Her father dragged the boy away. 'A fine husband you'd make, can't you see that you've upset her? I think you'd better leave and take your cloak with you.'

The boy moved towards the door of the cottage. 'You can keep the cloak, and when you believe enough in my love, Meinir, then I will hear your answer and then you will marry me.'

As the boy opened the cottage door, Meinir's father just behind him, there was a noise in the cottage. It was like the song of a skylark, it was so light and airy. Meinir's father and the boy turned round. Meinir was standing, the cloak wrapped around her shoulders.

'I will marry you,' Meinir said.

The boy ran over to her and hugged her.

Meinir's father was shocked. 'What kind of trickery is this?' he demanded.

'Not trickery, true love,' the boy said. 'Didn't you know that true love is the strongest magic of all?'

And it is.

Meinir and Prince Giffard, (for the boy was indeed a prince), were married as soon as Meinir was recovered. Their wedding day was celebrated throughout the kingdom with feasting and merry-making and everyone was happy.

Meinir's father came to live with Meinir and Giffard at their castle and he was well looked after for the rest of his life. He never again went back to the cottage in the woods, but it was kept as a resting place for weary travellers to spend the night and became known as a place of refuge.

When Giffard became King, he reigned for more than forty years and he was a true and kind ruler. Meinir was by his side as his queen. And the pair were inseparable and their devotion was true.

Meinir is a Welsh name meaning delicate, slender maiden.

Giffard is a Germanic name meaning stern ruler.

THE ORPHAN CHILD

THE ORPHAN CHILD

'An orphan child, an orphan child, that's what I am,'
Gissie said to herself each day, reminding herself that
she was always alone.

She was twelve years old and had been on her
own for three years. For eight years she'd had a father
and a mother and for one year longer, her mother; but for
three years she had been alone, no family, no friends, no
one.

And then it happened, one day, someone
happened to knock on her door.

Now Gissie lived in the woods and nobody
passed by her cottage, no one; so that someone should be
passing by was odd to say the least.

Gissie opened the door at the sound of the knocking and was amazed to see an old woman standing there.

'Ah, young lady, may I come in? I've been travelling long and have a while further to go before I reach my home. I am so tired. I need to rest for a while.'

Gissie took pity on the old woman and bid her come in and sit down.

Now the old woman had a kindly face and was soon chatting away to Gissie. After a while the old woman said, 'What is your name, child?'

'Gissie.'

'Are you alone, Gissie?'

'Yes. I am an orphan.'

The old woman looked Gissie up and down.

'Would you like to come and live with me? I have a house in the town, and as you can see, I am old. I could do with some help, and if you came along with me, well then neither of us need be alone anymore.'

'I don't think I can leave. Everything that is here reminds me of my mother and father.'

'You would still have your home; of course you would, and you could visit whenever you wished. You wouldn't be doing chores all the time.'

'But you don't know me.'

'I can see from your face that you are kind and honest, and that is all I need to know,'

'What if we don't get on, or I do something wrong and upset you?'

'If we don't get on, you may leave.'

Gissie looked around her home. The decision didn't take long to make.

'I'll come with you,' she said. And so, a little while later, Gissie and the old woman set off on their journey.

When they arrived at the old woman's house, Gissie stood back in amazement. The old woman was obviously rich. This house was larger than any other house Gissie had ever seen. Once inside, the old woman showed Gissie to her room. It was light and beautifully furnished.

'Make yourself comfortable, and then come downstairs. I'll brew us some tea,' the old woman said.

A little while later Gissie was downstairs, taking tea with the old woman.

'Is your room to your liking?' the old woman asked.

'It's perfect,' Gissie answered.

'Good, and your tea, how is that?'

'Perfect.'

'I'm glad you like it,' the old woman answered, 'because that's the way I like my tea. That's the way you must make it for me each day. Now, just one more thing, and you must listen and follow these instructions exactly. The flight of stairs opposite your room leads up to my room; you must never climb the stairs to come and find me, never. You may call up the stairs and I will answer you, but you must *not* climb the stairs.'

Just then, as the old woman was speaking, a black cat came into the room and jumped onto the old woman's lap. 'Ah, come lie down my precious,' the old woman said. The cat comfied itself on her lap and began to purr.

'He's lovely,' Gissie said.

'He is indeed. His name's Jabez, but as friendly as he looks, do not touch him. No one can ever get as close to him as me. He won't allow it.'

'I see,' Gissie said.

'I hope you do. If you do, we shall all get on famously. Now, drink up your tea and I'll show you where the kitchen is.'

Gissie drank her tea and then followed the old woman through the house. When they arrived at the kitchen the old woman said, 'This is where your work will be done. I have one cooked meal a day, at one o'clock. That is when you too, will eat.'

'Will there be any cleaning of the house to do, dusting and sweeping?'

'No, only your own room. Everything else will be taken care of.'

'I understand,' Gissie said.

'I hope you do,' the old woman said.

'What do you like to eat?' Gissie asked.

'Whatever you cook, meat, fish or fowl, I will eat it. You will be able to manage that?'

'Yes, of course,' Gissie replied.

For the next few weeks everything went well. Gissie cooked whatever was in the kitchen, although where the supplies came from, she couldn't make out, as no one from the town; the butcher, baker or greengrocer, seemed to deliver. This puzzled Gissie, but she didn't speak of it to the old woman. As far as she could see it was none of her business, and anyway, Gissie rarely saw the old woman. The only living thing she did see regularly was the old woman's cat, Jabez, and he was no company at all.

After a few more weeks, things changed. Previously, the old woman had come down the stairs to collect her meal. Now Gissie was told to put the food on a tray at the bottom of the stairs. Gissie did as she was asked, and although she never saw the old woman, she heard her footsteps on the stairs, and on checking, would see that the tray of food had gone.

A few more weeks went by and things changed again. The old woman didn't come for the food and Gissie became worried. After a few days of the same behaviour, Gissie called up the stairs to the old woman. The old woman replied, saying, 'I'm not hungry, eat yours and give mine to the cat.'

Gissie did as the old woman said and took the tray of food into the kitchen to give to the cat. This went on for weeks, eventually Gissie asked, 'Should I get a doctor for you? Are you ill?'

'No,' the old woman said, 'just do as you are told, eat yours and give mine to the cat.'

Gissie did as the old woman asked and never questioned her again, but as time went on, Gissie was wishing that she had stayed in her own cottage. She would talk to the old woman and tell her that she wanted to leave her employ. Her mind made up, Gissie decided that she would speak to the old woman the following day.

The next day was the same as all the days before. Gissie took the old woman's meal to the bottom of the stairs. 'Lunch is ready. Shall I leave it for you?'

'No,' replied the old woman, 'eat yours and give mine to the cat.'

Gissie took the food to the kitchen and fed the meal to the cat, Jabez.

This could not go on any longer. Gissie went up the stairs and stood at the foot of the staircase that was opposite her room. She paused. If she went up the stairs she would be disobeying her employer. On the other hand she was leaving, so what difference would it make?

Gissie started up the staircase. At the top of the stairs was the door to the old woman's room. It was closed. Gissie could hear voices. One was a man's voice, of that she was sure. She touched the door handle. The door was locked. Gissie bent and looked through the keyhole. The old woman was dancing round in a circle. She was dressed all in black and her cat was with her. The cat Gissie had only minutes earlier given food to.

Gissie watched, transfixed. The cat Jabez grew taller and was standing on his back legs. His front legs became arms. The cat stood next to the old woman and was as tall as a man. Gissie, still watching, looked on in horror as the cat's ears became horns. This cat was as dark as the devil himself. The cat's fur became thick and woolly and he grew taller and taller. He was a cat no more.

'Ah, Jabez', the old woman said, and the two of them began to dance. Round and round, faster and faster.

Gissie stepped back and crept as quietly and as quickly as she could, down the stairs. She made her way through the hall to the front door and left the house, never to return.

Gissie never told anyone what she had seen and she never saw the old woman again.

The name Jabez means causing pain and/or grief.

Gissie is a made-up name. The nearest name to it is

perhaps Gisela, which means 'pledged'.

THE SEVEN STONES

THE SEVEN STONES

By the river of Calacade, deep in the valley known as
Blott, there were seven stones. These stones had been in
the valley as long as anyone living there could
remember. There were stories passed on through the
generations about these stones, and some would say that
they were dropped by a giant as he ran away from a fight
with another giant, or that a giant's wife had dropped
them as she carried them in her pinny, on her way to
make a pathway across the river. There were others that
said an imp had laid them there and that if only a riddle
could be solved, then they would lead to a miser's hoard;
but generally the feeling was that they were just stones
that happened to be where they were due to a mystery of
nature, and that was that.

There were some from the village in the valley who avoided walking near the stones, and woe betide them if they were to inadvertently step on one of the seven, but these folk were in the minority. Abel Roberts was one such person.

Abel had lived in the village all his life, and his father before him, and his father before that. He walked past the stones on his way to school when he was a lad, passed them to go to church, passed them when he went to buy provisions from the shop. Everything in Blott was situated beyond the stones.

When Abel grew to be a man he decided that he would build himself a house beyond the stones, so he could be near to everything that Blott had to offer, which wasn't very much, truth be told.

He would build himself a home beyond the stones and take himself a wife. Abel had seen a girl in the village, a girl with flaxen hair and ruby-red lips. Her name was Joanna, and he decided from the first moment that he set eyes on her that she should be his wife. Abel was a man of few words, as was his father before him and his father before that, but this did not bother Abel. He knew what the task in hand was and he set about it.

Now Abel worked for the local sawmill owner, Jim Harold, a kind and generous man who thought a lot of Abel. In fact he treated Abel as his son, never having married or had any children of his own. One day Jim said to Abel, 'What is it that bothers you so?'

'Nothing', replied Abel.

'Nothing? I'm sure it's more than nothing, why your face is longer than the face of my old plough horse and you say there's nothing the matter with you?'

'Well, maybe one thing.'

'And what's that?'

'I want to build myself a house.'

'I see,' said Jim.

'Yes, I want a house this side of the stones.'

'I guess you'd better get ahead and build it then. That's all you can do.'

'I've no money to buy bricks.'

'You save as much as you can. If you've fifty pounds in three months, I'll supply all the bricks you need.'

'Really?' Abel said.

'Really,' Jim replied.

The time flew by, and in three months Abel had the fifty pounds. He took it with him to the sawmill and gave it to Jim Harold.

'What do your folks say about your house building aspirations?'

'They're all for it,' Abel replied.

'That's good. I own a plot of land 1 mile away from the sawmill. I've marked it out. It's yours. After work you can go and look at it. Take your father with you; you'll need help in the building of a house. If you like it you can start building as soon as you like. You'll find everything you need is there.'

Abel did as he was told, and one month to the day he took on the land, his house was finished. Now all he needed was to take him a wife. On his next free day he would go to the village and speak to Joanna.

Abel spotted Joanna as soon as he reached the market place. How could anyone miss her? It would have been impossible, she was so much prettier than the other girls in the village; or at least that was what Abel thought. And today he had a plan, first he would go to the alehouse and buy himself some courage, and then he would do it, he would seek out Joanna and ask her to marry him.

Abel finished his drink and went back to the market place. He saw Joanna sitting on a seat that faced out towards the fields and the river. He walked over to her. 'Joanna', he said.

'Hello Abel, what do you want?'

'I've come to ask you a question?'

'A question? That sounds interesting.'

'Maybe?'

'Abel, you are the funniest person! What is it you want to say to me?'

'It's this. Marry me!'

'Marry you? I won't marry anyone who can't get me the best things in life, a home, servants, fine clothes. I'm sorry Abel.'

'I have a house, Joanna.'

'And where is this house?'

'Behind the sawmill.'

'Behind the sawmill? You would expect me to marry you, and then on top of that come and live in a house behind the sawmill!'

'Are you saying no?'

'I am. Goodbye Abel.' And with that, Joanna got up from her seat and went and mingled with the people in the market place. Abel stayed where he was for a while and tried to gather his thoughts. How could he have been so stupid as to fall for somebody who was as inconsiderate as Joanna! He would not be so blind again.

That evening Abel decided to call at the home of his mother and father. He had to walk past the seven stones to get there. As he came level with the first stone, he heard a voice, 'Come to me, come to me,' it said. Abel looked round, confused and confounded. There was not another soul on the path. As he stood, he heard the voice again. 'Come to me, come to me.'

'Who is that? Who's there?'

'It is just the stones, just the stones.'

'But I hear a voice, a human voice.'

'So you do, so you do. It is I calling out to you.'

'Who are you?'

'I am the largest of the seven stones, the one you are standing next to.'

'And?'

'First you must come to me.'

'I cannot, no one must tread near the stones.'

'That's all made up stories. All made up stories. Come closer, come to me.'

'Why?'

'I'll make you rich.'

'But who are you?'

'I was the queen of this valley, turned to stone with six of my courtiers for being free-willed, free-spirited.'

'How can you speak?'

'It is the thirteenth of the month, this is my day. It is one hundred years since the deed was done to me.'

'And?'

73

'And this is my one chance to be free. Abel, you are my chance to live again.'

'Why should I believe you?'

'Because I am telling the truth.'

'But I can't see you.'

'If you do as I say you will be wealthy beyond your dreams.'

'And I will live?'

'Of course you will live! I just need you to help me break away from this miserable curse.'

'Who cursed you?'

'Abel, you don't say much, but for a man of few words you ask too many questions. Will you help me?'

'No harm will befall me...or my family?'

'No harm will come to you.'

'Promise?'

'I promise.'

'What do I have to do?'

'Stand on my back, and walk down the line of all the stones. When you are on the last stone, turn round three times and then say these words, 'The moon shines bright, lights up the night, the sun lights up the day.'

Abel walked down the line of stones and did as he was bid.

The stone spoke again. 'Now you must do this; take some earth from next to the stone and drop a few grains of soil onto each stone as you walk back to me, when you are standing on my stone place a few grains on my stone and then throw the rest of the earth over your left shoulder.'

'It was the devil himself who cursed you!' Abel said.

'It was, will you still promise to help me?'

'I will.'

Abel did as he was bid and when he had thrown the soil over his left shoulder he said.

'What now?'

'Now you must say three times, 'Awake our queen, awake.'

Abel completed the third of his tasks, and after a few moments he heard a rustling behind him. He turned and was amazed to see six courtiers coming to life from the very stones themselves. They looked stunned and jaded, but when they saw they were in their home valley they were pleased. Pleased to be alive again.

The largest of the seven stones spoke again, 'Courtiers, go into the woods and find your horses. They will be where you left them.'

The courtiers went into the woods. The stone spoke again, 'Abel. It's just we two now, please, get off my back!'

'Oh, sorry,' Abel said as he stepped off the largest of the stones.

Almost at once a beautiful girl appeared from the earth. Her hair was as black as night, but her eyes; her eyes were the most magnificent blue, and her lips, her lips were ruby-red. In an instant, Abel thought of Joanna.

'Why do you bother about the girl from the village? She would bring you nothing but sadness. She is spiteful and thoughtless, not the one for you Abel,' the girl said.

'I know that, she turned me down.'

'I would not turn you down, were you to ask.'

'I cannot ask you. You are a queen.'

'I am, but not what you think. I was queen of the May.'

'But your courtiers, the ones who came to life?'

'Dressing up for the occasion.'

'Do all women lie?' Abel asked.

'To get what they want. It has been known.'

'So there is no wealth?'

'Wealth can also be of the soul, not just in gold to be counted.'

'I have been made a fool of.'

'You have shown kindness to another; that is not foolishness.'

'Not in your eyes, but in mine.'

'I'm sorry you feel that way, but in any case, you gave me my life back, so thank-you for that. Now I shall be on my way.'

'Where are you going?'

'Wherever there are a few good folk. I am sure such a place still exists.'

'It might do. I bid you good luck.'

'Thank-you Abel, and I give you my good luck also, and may you have all you wish and desire.'

'Just one thing, what is your name?'

'Elaine.'

And with that, Abel and Elaine turned and went their separate ways.

Abel stayed the night with his mother and father, and the next day went to his home behind the sawmill, where he lived for many happy years. He never did marry, but he wasn't lonely, he had his own company and he enjoyed it. And when Jim Harold died he left the mill and all his land to Abel. Abel became a wealthy man in his own right; the wealthiest man in the village.

Joanna married, and for wealth, as she said she would; but her husband was a drunkard and treated her badly and soon she realised that the finer things in life weren't always what they seemed.

No one ever saw Elaine again, and sometimes Abel wondered whether he had ever seen her at all, or whether it had all been a dream.

One thing was for certain though. The seven stones were still there, and from that day to this, no one ever mentioned hearing them speak; and Abel never mentioned it either.

MIRROR
MIRROR

MIRROR, MIRROR

She picked up the mirror that lay on the dressing table. It was a plainish, wooden-framed mirror with a tortoiseshell back. The handle of the mirror had tiny rosebuds painted onto it. They were to add some prettiness, yet somehow they didn't. As she turned the glass to catch her reflection, she thought she caught sight of something, no, not something, someone. Someone was watching her. She turned quickly. There was no one there. Of course there wasn't, there couldn't be, could there? She was in her bedroom and she was alone; and yet for that split-second, if she had been asked, she would have replied, '*yes, yes, there was someone there*'.

Her image checked, she replaced the mirror on the dressing table and went downstairs to where her husband was waiting for her. Today was their wedding anniversary. Seven years. Copper or wool. Copper or wool would have been traditional. He was always predictable; usually predictable. The mirror wasn't the expected gift.

'Do you like the mirror? I thought you would. It's old you see, and I know you like old things, and I thought, with the rosebuds on the handle, painted on, well, I know how you like flowers and so I thought it was the perfect gift. The woman in the shop said I could change it if it wasn't suitable, but I knew as soon as I saw it that you would like it, that it was the ideal gift.'

'It's perfect. You chose well,' she lied. And off they went for dinner.

She didn't want to use the mirror, not after that evening, not after what had happened. Not after what she had seen; and she couldn't tell him, could she? Her thoughts were kept to herself, locked away inside. The thing was, she was intrigued by the mirror and what she thought she had seen. Intrigued and frightened at the same time. Who was it, who was it she had seen captured there for no more than a split-second? Of course it could just have been a trick of the light but instinct told her that it was something more. She was resolute in her decision and left the mirror face-down on the dressing table.

Three weeks passed. Three weeks. Three times seven. Three and seven. Magic numbers.

On the evening of that twenty-first day, she went up to bed, said goodnight to her husband and climbed the stairs. Later, as she was sitting at her dressing table, she turned to see him standing in the doorway.

'You startled me,' she said.

'I didn't mean to,' he replied, 'but my gift to you, the mirror, you never seem to use it. I just wondered, don't you like it?'

She picked up the mirror. 'Of course I like it, it's lovely.' And without looking into the glass she placed it back down on her dressing table. He watched her, he loved her and he sensed that something was wrong. Sensed that something had changed, but he didn't know why. 'I'll be up later. I'll just go and lock up,' he said.

The twenty-first night, three times seven. Seven, seven, seven. Lucky seven, seven for luck. Three, turn three times, circle the pin, stick it in. Three times seven.

She heard her husband's steps on the stairs, listened as they became quieter. Listened until she could hear them no more.

She sat for a moment longer, looked at the mirror, the plain mirror with the wooden frame and tortoiseshell back and the rosebuds painted on the handle. She knew that her strength had gone, that her resolve was lost, knew that she must pick up the mirror and look into the glass. She looked at herself in the mirror, and as she saw herself reflected in the glass, she found that she was drawn to look deep into the glass; to look beyond herself and her own reflection, to look at what else was reflected in the mirror. She saw a face, not hers, a face reflected beyond her own. Another face in another room. Still holding on to the mirror she turned, there was no one else there. When she turned to look in the mirror again, it was blank, like a still pool, dark and deep, nothing to see, not even her own reflection. She put the mirror face-down on the dressing table and vowed not to look into the glass again. She stood up, walked over to the bed, turned down the covers and slipped inside. She didn't hear her husband come to bed. She went straight to sleep. And she didn't dream, not of what had just happened, not of mirrors and rosebuds or the reflection of others, of none of those things did she dream, but she slept, deeply, peacefully, until the morning.

When three months had passed, twelve weeks, three times four, lock the door, strike of the clock, lock, lock, lock.

When it was three months passed she was minded to pick up the mirror again. So she picked it up and saw her own reflection, looked past it, looked past her own room and beyond, into another room, saw her own face disappear, saw another reflected, not her own. And so she turned around and saw a figure standing there, in her room, yet it wasn't her room, it was another place she saw. It was unfamiliar but not frightening. And she didn't speak, not her, nor the figure; no one spoke, not one to the other. She turned around to the dressing table and it was her own, and she placed the mirror face-down on the dressing table. Turned again to see her own bedroom. The figure had gone, she was alone.

'You're quiet, lately,' her husband said.

'Nothing much to say,' she replied. And it was true. Since their anniversary and '*the gift*', they had started to drift apart. She didn't know what to say to him. Didn't want to speak to him, not anymore.

Five months and one week, twenty-one weeks. Three times seven. Three and seven; magic numbers.

She had ceased talking to her husband. She spent a lot of time sitting by her dressing table. She spent a lot of time looking in the mirror. The plain mirror with the tortoiseshell back and the rosebuds painted on the handle. The mirror that no longer showed her reflection, or her room. The mirror that showed another room, another person reflected there. Not her, not anymore.

And while she was there, she would speak to the woman in the mirror; tell her things, her thoughts and fancies, and the secrets that her husband would never know.

Three times seven. Seven, seven, seven. Lucky seven. Seven for luck. Three, turn three times, circle the pin, stick it in. Twenty-one. Three times seven.

And then tonight. Tonight she sat alone by the dressing table. Sat alone and picked up the mirror, looked into it, beyond the glass and through to the other room, the other face.

'Turn around, look at me.'

She turned. The room was not her room. The figure in her room was familiar to her; it was the woman in the mirror who had visited before.

'Come to me, walk to me.'

And she did. And she passed through the figure and felt herself begin to spin, her head was light, she was dizzy. She felt herself going, leaving all that she knew, but knowing then that nothing else really mattered. It was this moment that was important, and she let it take her. And she was no more. She was in another place, another place where no one would find her.

And later, when her husband sat wishing that his wife would return and wondering where she could be

85

and why she had left him, he glanced at the dressing table and saw the mirror; the plainish, wooden-framed mirror with the tortoiseshell back and rosebuds painted on the handle, and he picked it up. It was then that he thought he saw her, for a moment reflected in the glass, but he dismissed it and considered it a trick of the light.

ACKNOWLEDGEMENTS

Thanks to all the people who have helped me to put this collection together; you know who you are.

Thanks also to the editors of *Cloudbursts*, an anthology in which *CROW SONG* first appeared.

ABOUT THE AUTHOR

Margaret Holbrook grew up in Cheshire, where she still lives. Her work has been published in anthologies and magazines and broadcast on radio.

She writes fiction, plays and poetry.
In 2014 her play, *The Supper Party*, was a finalist in the *'Grand Words'* competition, run in conjunction with the Grand Theatre, Blackpool.
Her short story, *Our Brian*, was longlisted for the BBC Radio 4 programme, 'Opening Lines', in the same year.

Website: **www.margaretholbrookwrites.weebly.com**

OTHER BOOKS BY MARGARET HOLBROOK

Watching and other Stories, *Short stories, fiction.*

Cul De Sac Tales, *Humour, fiction.*

Hobby Horses Will Dance, *Poetry.*